Friends!

Friends!

by Elaine Scott
photographs by Margaret Miller

Atheneum Books for Young Readers
NEW YORK · LONDON · TORONTO · SYDNEY · SINGAPORE

Atheneum Books for Young Readers
An imprint of Simon & Schuster Children's Publishing Division
1230 Avenue of the Americas
New York, New York 10020

The photographer would like to thank everyone who appears in this book
for their patience and generosity:

Jacqueline Avens, Zachary Bleckner, Charlotte Bradley, Mwanzaa Brown,
Emily Buse, Esther Yukiko Carey, Christopher & Maggie Confrey, Monique Davis,
Matthew Dunne, Gabrielle Ferguson, Billy & Whitney Ford, Paul Gladstone, Amos & Charlie Goldstein,
Tara & Thomas Ginty, Ben Jacobson, Michelle Long, Ariel Maiello, Kaitlyn, Brian & Taylor Moore,
Zachary Muller, Molli, Casey, Jillian & Michael Olbermann, Tara St. Onge, Travis Reuther,
Stephen Tanico, and Tyler Youvon.

Book design by Nina Barnett

The text of this book is set in Meta Black.

Printed in Hong Kong
10   8   6   4   2   1   3   5   7   9

Library of Congress Cataloging-in-Publication Data
Scott, Elaine, 1940-
Friends! / by Elaine Scott; photographs by Margaret Miller.—1st ed.
p.   cm.   ill
Summary: Text and photographs introduce some friends and the activities they share and provide
discussion of how friends can help each other, share secrets, and solve their disagreements.
ISBN 0-689-82105-0
1. Friendship—Juvenile literature. [1. Friendship.]
I. Miller, Margaret, 1945-   II. Title.
BJ1533.F8S34   2000
177.62—dc21   99-10357

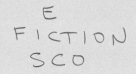

FIRST
EDITION

For my friend Margie, with love
—E.S.

For Elaine, my friend in work and play
—M.M.

Making friends is part of growing up. When you were little, the only people you knew were members of your family, but as you grew, your world grew bigger, too.

Now that you are older, friendship—
having friends and being a friend—
is more and more important.

Friends are people who like each other.

Some friends play together every day at school. Others may see each other once a week; at soccer, for example. Some people may have a lot of friends, and others may have just a few. Numbers are not important. Friendship is. Friends simply enjoy being with each other.

What are the names of your friends?
Where did you meet them?

Taylor and Gabrielle are friends. The two girls like to skate together. Gabrielle says, "I help Taylor put on her skates, and she helps me when I fall down.

It doesn't matter who's a better skater. We have fun."

B.J., Chris, and Zachary like to build with Legos. Usually each boy builds something by himself, but sometimes they work together. It was B.J.'s idea to make a harbor filled with pirate ships.

Charlotte and Paul like to pretend they are chefs. Charlotte says, "We play it's our restaurant. I make the coffee, and Paul fixes the vegetables."

What things do you do with your friends? Are you friends with both boys and girls?

Besides sharing similar interests, friends can also introduce each other to new things. When Taylor learned how to make greeting cards on her family's computer, she wanted to show Gabrielle how to make them, too.

And when Gabrielle took gymnastics, she showed Taylor how to do a cartwheel. "It's not that hard, but you have to practice," said Gabrielle.

What new things have you learned from your friends?

Friends share our good times, and make them even better.

Mwanzaa likes to make cookies, and Zachary likes to help him.

Cookies taste twice as good when you make them with a friend.

Later, Mwanzaa said, "Maybe you can spend the night at my house tomorrow. I'll ask my mom."

Friends plan the things they want to do together. The more time they spend together, the more their friendship grows.

Friends share bad times, too, making them easier.

Maggie and Matthew love to play

basketball. When Maggie

broke her arm, Matthew

knew they wouldn't

be able to play ball

for a while.

Matthew told

Maggie, "We

can play

other games

until your arm

gets better."

Have you helped a friend during a bad time?

Friends often share their friendship with others.

Monique and Ariel are best friends. When Tara moved into the house across the street, Monique said, "Let's go over and meet her. Maybe she'd like to play." Ariel said, "That's a great idea. I remember when I moved here and you were nice to me."

Have you ever included a new person in your group of friends?

Friends trust each other and accept each other just the way they are.

Chris loves to go swimming with his friends, Zachary and B.J., but jumping off the high diving board scares him. When Chris was alone with B.J., he said, "I really don't like jumping off the high board, but please don't tell anybody. I'm embarrassed."

How would you feel if a friend told your secret?

All friends have disagreements from time to time,
and anger can test friendships. Esther and Emily often play games,
but when Esther won two games in a row, Emily was angry.
"This is a dumb game!" she shouted.

Esther said, "Let's play with my hamster, instead."

When Jacqueline wanted to see one film and Kaitlyn a different one,
they decided what to see by flipping a coin. Jacqueline won.
"We'll see your movie next Saturday," she said.

How have you and your friends solved disagreements?

All friends have disagreements. But some people seem disagreeable most of the time. They pick on certain people and tease, bully, or even fight with them.

Mike's next-door neighbor, Jim, was mean most of the time. But when it was time for Mike's birthday party, suddenly Jim was friendly. Mike didn't want to invite Jim to his party, but he didn't want to be mean, either.

Mike's mother understood. "It's good you want to be kind to people," she said. "But it's hard to be a friend to Jim right now, because he doesn't understand what being a friend is all about. You have the right to choose your friends, and who will come to your party."

What would you do if you were Mike?

It is important to choose friends who make you feel good about yourself, but it is also important for friends to tell you if they think you are making a mistake.

Charlie didn't understand the math homework. After school, he saw his friend Amos. "I couldn't do the math assignment. Can I copy your paper?"

"No way!" said Amos. "That's cheating. Let me show you how to work the problems."

Have you ever told a friend "no" if they asked you to do something you shouldn't?

Your friends know a lot about you.

Whether you're feeling
silly or serious, friends
understand your moods
and respect them.

They celebrate with you in good times,

and sympathize with you in bad times.

As a friendship grows, friends know when to talk and when to listen.

Friends are more valuable than special sneakers, or jackets, or anything else people can buy with money. Friends like this are a little like members of your family.

Think about your friends. Why are they special to you?

A Note to Parents

Child psychologists have long said that play is the "work" of childhood. Part of that work is learning how to build and sustain friendships. Of course, children approach friendships differently at different ages. Very young children generally understand friendships as existing for today, and a "best" friend is the person they are playing with at the moment. However, by first grade most children are beginning to grasp the concept that a friendship equals a relationship. This book is aimed at children who are entering the middle stages of childhood, roughly five to nine years old, though certainly its concepts can be applied to older and younger children as well.

Child development specialists say that by the time children reach school age, most are able to understand broad principles of equality, such as treating others as they would like to be treated; nevertheless, their first forays into friendships can be stormy. At this age a child is often competitive and wants to win—not just one game, but all the games. Emily and Esther's story can provide an opportunity for discussion not only about resolving disagreements, but competitiveness in general.

Early friendships are often possessive, and the thought of asking another person to join a twosome is difficult. "Only two can play," is a frequently heard playground refrain. Sharing the story of Monique, Tara, and Ariel encourages discussion about whether it is easy, or difficult, to invite new people to join a group and allows parents to share their values of inclusiveness in a casual way.

Of course, not all children are likable all of the time, and dealing with a bully is one of the most distressing situations children (and their parents) face. "No one likes a tattletale" is one of childhood's mantras, and too many children suffer in silence rather than tell their troubles to an understanding adult. Jim, Mike, and the birthday party may provide an opening for discussion that helps children understand the

difference between tattling and talking constructively about what is bothering them. That discussion could convey the idea that tattling is an attempt to get another person in trouble, perhaps for no reason at all. But telling an adult when someone is bullying or hurting another person is not tattling. It is simply telling the truth.

By the middle of childhood, boys and girls are capable of forming friendships that are true two-way relationships. Around the ages of eight and nine, children are concerned with what their friends do, as well as what their friends think. Loyalty among friends becomes extremely important, and betrayal can turn a friend into an enemy—a word that creeps into the vocabulary of eight-to-nine-year-olds. Chris, Zachary, and B.J. and the high dive may provoke lively discussion on this topic.

Eventually, children reach a stage when the opinion of their friends weighs equally—and perhaps more—than the opinion of their parents or their teachers. The story of Charlie, Amos, and the math homework is an example of the kind of pressure children face every day. An adult could expand on that anecdote to talk about how Charlie would really feel about handing in homework he hadn't done himself. Or how Amos would feel if he allowed Charlie to copy his work. Contrast their feelings with Ariel's and Monique's after they invited Tara to play, and emphasize the fact that our friends should bring out the best in us, not the worst.

Childhood friendships form the basis for social skills that will carry a child through life. Though nothing can replace the value system a child learns within the family, we hope this book will lead to lively discussions that help young readers learn how to become the kind of friends who care, comfort, and, when necessary, confront.